A Handful of Sunshine

Melanie Eclare

Ragged Bears
Brooklyn, New York • Milborne Wick, Dorset

Tilda loves growing sunflowers.

For Tilda

Published in the United States by Ragged Bears, Inc., 413 Sixth Avenue, Brooklyn, New York 11215
www.raggedbears.com

Originally published in Great Britain in 1999 by Ragged Bears Publishing, Milborne Wick, Sherborne, Dorset DT9 4PW

CIP Data is available.

First American edition. Printed and bound in China.

ISBN 1-929927-14-2

2 4 6 8 10 9 7 5 3 1

These are the seeds she bought with her pocket money.

The best time to start growing
sunflowers is in the spring,
so in March, Tilda begins to dig.

She prepares a flower bed by clearing the weeds and then making a hole for each seed. Then, she takes the seeds out of the packet.

SUNFLOWER
Morgan

SUNFLOWER

One by one she pops a
seed in each hole she's
dug in her new flower
bed.

Suddenly Tilda jumps with surprise...

A baby toad has come to see what she's doing!

She carefully puts him under a big leaf.

Now it's time to water her seeds...

After ten weeks, Tilda's
seeds have grown into
strong and healthy plants.
Every day they grow
bigger...

and bigger...

and bigger...

until they reach high up in the sky.

Tilda's seeds are now
beautiful sunflowers!

At the end of the summer,
Tilda climbs a ladder to
pick the head of the fattest,
best flower.

Tilda pulls all the seeds out of the old flower, and now she has her own sunflower seeds to grow for next year.

Growing Instructions

Wait till a warm day in April or early May, then find a suitable patch of ground with plenty of space for the sunflowers to grow.

Prepare the soil by raking it over.

Make a hole with your finger, drop one seed in, and then make another hole nearby - about two widths of your hand apart - and drop in the next seed.

Make as many holes and plant as many seeds as you can! The seeds will start to appear in two to three weeks.

When they're six inches high, they'll be getting crowded, so you'll need to pull out some plants. Each plant needs a lot of space! They should be one foot (ask a grown-up) away from each other.

The plants will grow to be very big - maybe up to ten feet tall!

When they're grown, you can pick the head...

...and keep the seeds in a safe place to plant next year.